The Day that REPEATED ITSELF

Written by Chris Callaghan and Zoë Clarke

Illustrated by Amit Tayal

Collins

Shinoy and the Chaos Crew

When Shinoy downloads the Chaos Crew app on his phone, a glitch in the system gives him the power to summon his TV heroes into his world.

With the team on board, Shinoy can figure out what dastardly plans the red-eyed S.N.A.I.R., a Super Nasty Artificial Intelligent Robot, has come up with, and save the day.

1 The cat

Shinoy was going to play football with Toby. As he left his house and turned right, Mr Blake waved at him from across the road. "Hi, Shinoy."

Dad and Myra drove by in the Relic 500. Myra waved out of the window and shouted, "Bye, Shinoy."

Shinoy wasn't looking where he was going, and fell over next door's cat.

When he got up, he found himself back in front of his house.

"That's weird." He pressed the app on his phone. "Call to Action, Chaos Crew!"

Mustang Harry, Chaos Crew super dog, appeared in
a flash of light.

"Shinoy! How may I assist?"

"I'm not sure," Shinoy said. "I was walking to
the park, I fell over a cat, and I suddenly appeared
back at my house."

Harry gave Shinoy a sniff. "I can smell the cat!
And something else ... you and an echo of you."

"An echo?"

"Yes. Like a faded version of you, as well as
the *real* you. Show me the cat."

"The cat's probably gone by now," Shinoy said.

They left the house. They turned right.

Mr Blake waved.
"Hi, Shinoy!"

Myra waved.
"Bye, Shinoy!"

"That happened last time!" Shinoy said.

Harry looked at Shinoy. "Interesting."

Suddenly, Harry stopped. "Cat!" he barked. "Jump!"

Shinoy jumped and the cat ran underneath him.

"Whew!" Shinoy breathed.

They crossed the road and Shinoy saw a broken bike. It was *his* bike!

He picked it up, and found himself back in front of his house. Harry had gone.

2 The bike

Shinoy pressed the Chaos Crew app, but this time Bug appeared in a flash of light.

"Shinoy! What needs fixing?"

"I don't know!" Shinoy said. "Maybe me?"

Bug peered at him. "Ooh, I'm seeing two echoes. Interesting."

"That's what Harry said. Only it was one echo before."

Bug frowned. "Show me the problem."

They left the house. They turned right.

There was Mr Blake.
"Hi, Shinoy!"

And Myra.
"Bye, Shinoy!"

Shinoy's phone made a BARK sound.

He remembered to J U M P over the cat.

They found his broken bike and Bug handed Shinoy
a screwdriver.

Shinoy tightened the pedals.

Shinoy got on his bike, with Bug on the back, and raced round the corner. They crashed into Shinoy's head teacher, Mr Amitri.

"Cycling without care, Shinoy?" Mr Amitri said.
"And with a passenger! I'm going to confiscate
this bicycle!"

Mr Amitri grabbed the bicycle.

Shinoy found himself back outside his house.
Bug had gone.

3 The map

Shinoy pressed the Chaos Crew app. Now, super-sneaky Lazlo appeared in a flash of light.

"Ooh, echoes!" Lazlo began.

"That's what Bug and Harry said!"

"Looks like three. You've done the same thing three times before."

"I know!" Shinoy said.

"You're going round in a loop."

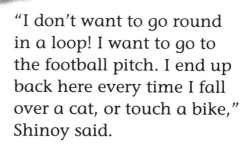

"I don't want to go round in a loop! I want to go to the football pitch. I end up back here every time I fall over a cat, or touch a bike," Shinoy said.

"What went wrong this time?" Lazlo asked.

"I crashed into Mr Amitri!" Shinoy groaned.

They left the house. They turned right.

"Hi, Shinoy!"

"Bye, Shinoy!"

BARK from the phone.
J U M P over the cat.

Bug's screwdriver was
on the path! Shinoy
grabbed it and fixed
the bike. Again.

14

Lazlo got a large map from his pocket. "Let's go!"

Shinoy cycled round the corner, with Lazlo on the back of his bike. Lazlo let go of the map, which blew into Mr Amitri's face!

Shinoy swerved and raced up the hill.

"Ooh-er," Lazlo gulped.

"I don't believe it!" Shinoy said. It was S.N.A.I.R.! "I don't want to be stuck in a loop with him!"

S.N.A.I.R. fired lasers and Shinoy found himself back in front of his house. Lazlo had gone.

15

4 The shield

Shinoy pressed the Chaos Crew app. This time, Salama appeared.

"Don't tell me," he said. "Echoes? Probably four now."

"I have come to free you from your torment!" she vowed.

"Oh, good," Shinoy said, sarcastically, "but first we have to defeat S.N.A.I.R."

"I will vanquish him!"

"Fine by me," Shinoy said.

They left the house. They turned right.

"Hi, Shinoy!"

"Bye, Shinoy!"

BARK from the phone.
J U M P over the cat.

Grab the screwdriver.
Fix the bike.

Pick up the map. Swerve round Mr Amitri.

S.N.A.I.R. was waiting.

"You'll never get past my lasers, weaklings!"

Shinoy folded his arms. "We could if we went
a different way."

"That's not how this works! You try to pass and I'll fire
lasers at you!"

S.N.A.I.R. shot his lasers ... They bounced off Salama's
shield and hit S.N.A.I.R. in the chest.

"A mighty conquest!" Salama shouted as they raced down the path.

There was a bridge near the football pitch. But there was a plank loose and Shinoy was catapulted off his bike. He found himself back outside his house. Salama had gone.

Shinoy pressed the app on his phone. Merit appeared this time.

"Amigo! Do you –"

Shinoy screwed up his face. "Five echoes! I'm stuck in a never-ending loop!"

Merit smoothed his hair. "Do you need a hug?"

"No hugging! Let's go!"

They left the house. They turned right.

"Hi, Shinoy!"   "Bye, Shinoy!"

BARK from the phone.
J U M P over the cat.

Grab the screwdriver.
Fix the bike.

Pick up the map.
Swerve round
Mr Amitri.

Lift the shield.
Defeat S.N.A.I.R.

Shinoy and Merit got to the bridge. "There's a plank loose," Shinoy said.

Merit flexed his muscles. "Fear not! This calls for my superior strength."

Merit picked up a fallen branch and wedged it into the gap in the bridge.

Shinoy pedalled on, until they reached the football pitch.

"I've made it!" Shinoy laughed.

He touched the gate, and found himself back outside his house. Merit had gone.

6 The loop

"I was so close!" Shinoy shouted. He pressed the app on his phone. Ember appeared.

"Why are you shouting at the sky?" she asked. "And –"

"Yes, the echoes! Six! I'm never going to escape this loop!"

"What I was *going* to say was that loops go in sixes. Complete the final task and everything returns to normal."

"But I *can't* do it. The gate to the football pitch is really tall. I'd need to be able to fly to get over it – oh."

Ember smiled.

They left the house. They turned right.

"No!" Shinoy held up a hand when he saw Mr Blake and then Myra.

BARK! J U M P over the cat!

Screwdriver. Fix the bike.

Map. Swerve around
Mr Amitri.

Shield. Defeat S.N.A.I.R.

Branch. Fix the bridge.

They stood in front of the gate.
"It is quite tall, isn't it," Ember said,
unfolding her wings.

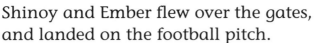

Shinoy and Ember flew over the gates, and landed on the football pitch.

Toby ran over. "That was quick! I only called you ten minutes ago."

"It feels like hours," Shinoy said.

"Hi, Ember! Is there an emergency?"

"Not now. I think we're all good."

Toby looked at Shinoy. "I think you forgot something."

"What?"

"The football! Do you want to go home and get it?"

Shinoy could see Ember trying not to laugh.

"Not this time."

Loop the loop!

Loop 1

Loop 2

Loop 3

Loop 4

Loop 5

Loop 6

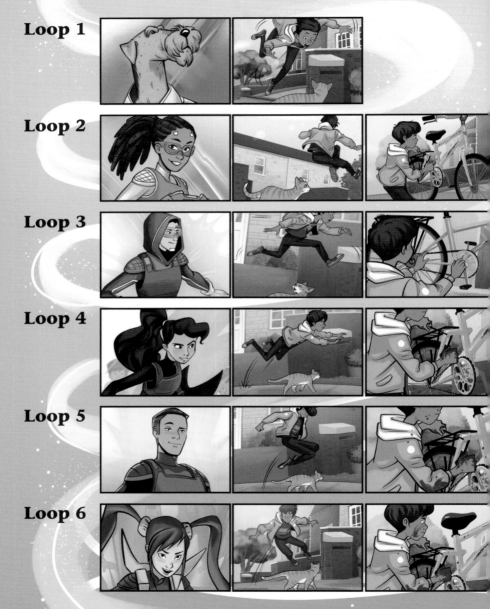

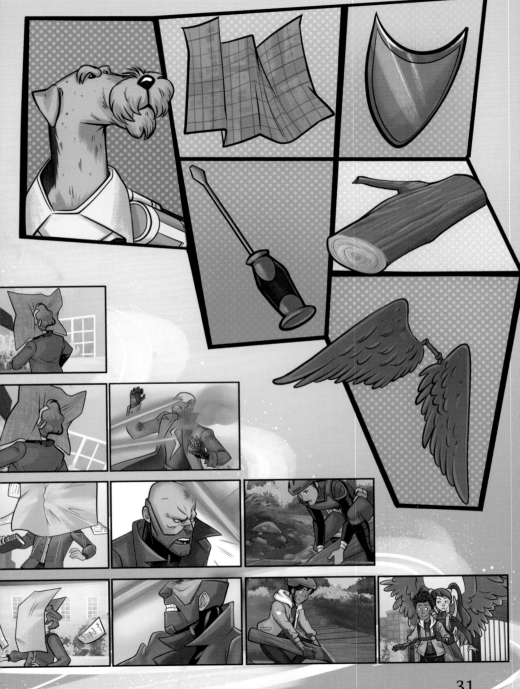

Ideas for reading

Written by Clare Dowdall, PhD
Lecturer and Primary Literacy Consultant

Reading objectives

- discuss the sequence of events in books and how items of information are related
- discuss and clarify the meanings of words, linking new meanings to known vocabulary
- draw on what they already know or on background information and vocabulary provided by the teacher
- check that the text makes sense to them as they read and correct inaccurate reading

Spoken language objectives

- use relevant strategies to build their vocabulary
- give well-structured descriptions and explanations

Curriculum links: PSHE – health and wellbeing: perseverance

Word count: 1,275

Interest words: echo, confiscate, torment, vanquish, conquest, catapulted

Resources: paper and pencils

Build a context for reading

- Look at the front cover and read the title *The Day that Repeated Itself.* Ask children to describe what they can see and to suggest how Shinoy is feeling. Create a list of words to describe his feelings, e.g. frustrated, annoyed, irritated ...
- Read the blurb together. Discuss what the mission means. Check that children understand *reliving the same scene again and again* and what being in *an endless loop* means.
- Check that children can decode the interest words. Ask children to look out for them as they read, and to try to work out what they mean in relation to the story.